For all the children who had to leave.
For all the children who had to stay behind.

P. G.-P.

For Tierry

L. Q.

Noor and Bobby

Written by **Praline Gay-Para**
Illustrations by **Lauranne Quentric**
Translated from the French by **Alyson Waters**

Restless Books
Brooklyn, New York

On the ground floor
of an apartment building,
a young boy named Noor
lives with his family.

But the rest of the homes are
now empty.
One by one the neighbors have left.

Only the lady on the sixth floor
still lives behind her apartment door.

Each morning, she walks her dog.

Each morning, Noor waits for them, patiently.

He names the dog Bobby, secretly.

When Bobby scampers by,
Noor pets his soft, warm nose

dreaming that some day they'll play
together, who knows?

One morning, the lady comes down from the sixth floor. A taxi is humming at the door.

"Oh! She's leaving, too, and taking Bobby away!

Don't go, **Bobby**!
Bobby, please stay!"

The taxi disappears down the road.
Bobby runs after it,
and Noor runs after Bobby.

"**Bobby**! Please come back to me!
I'm your friend, can't you see?"

"**Bobby,** did I lose you, too?"

Behind a wounded wall
Noor hears some sort of sound.
He strains his ears.

Could Bobby be here?

Noor climbs atop a pile of stones,
steps over rubble and then he sees

a bird in barbed wire, trapped.
Poor bird is going "flap, flap, flap."

And so, Noor sets the bird free.

Then Noor goes off again
to find his dearest friend.

"**Bobby**, **Bobby**, where are you?
Bobby, **Bobby**, can I come, too?"

Suddenly, Noor hears a squeaking sound.
He stops in his tracks and looks around.

"**Bobby** is that you?
Bobby, can you hear me, too?"

He walks beside a balcony
that's crumbled to the earth,
stumbles into a home with no walls,

and finds a cat who's just given birth.

Noor builds a shelter
for the cat and her kitties.
Then once again sets off
on his search of the city.

"**Bobby**! **Bobby**! Where are you?
Bobby! **Bobby**! Pleeeeze! Come back!"

Noor stops suddenly
atop a battered stairway.
He hears a growl not far away.
Could it be Bobby?

"**Bobby**, is that you?
Answer me!"

Noor steps down cautiously.

Noor enters an enormous room.
Everything is topsy-turvy,
covered in powdery dust.

Through a big gaping hole in the back wall,
he sees a lush green garden
where dogs and cats and birds
are lazing in the sun.

Bobby is there!

He barks, wags his tail, and jumps into Noor's arms.

"My **Bobby**! Here you are!
When we manage to leave this city, we'll leave together
and stay friends forever!
But for now, come with me!
When we get home, I'll give you treats."

ABOUT THE AUTHOR
Praline Gay-Para is a French-Lebanese storyteller, author, and actress. She's written numerous books for children and adults often based on her reflections about traditional folktales and life stories from Lebanon. In addition to her work as a writer and translator, Gay-Para also collaborates with the theater company Pavé Volubile to produce plays and live performances. She currently lives in Paris.

ABOUT THE ILLUSTRATOR
Lauranne Quentric is an illustrator based in Brittany, France. Since 2007 she has illustrated dozens of children's books and also creates intricate marionettes and sculptures for children's theater events. Her work has been featured in exhibitions of children's book illustration across France.

ABOUT THE TRANSLATOR
Alyson Waters is a translator of French and francophone literary fiction, art history, and children's literature. She is the recipient of several grants and was twice winner of the French-American Foundation Translation Prize, for Eric Chevillard's *Prehistoric Times* and for Jean Giono's *A King Alone*. Her translation of the children's book *The Tiger Prince* by Chen Jiang Hong was awarded the Prix Albertine Jeunesse in 2019. She lives in Brooklyn, New York.

ABOUT YONDER
Yonder is an imprint from Restless Books devoted to bringing the wealth of great stories from around the globe to English-reading children, middle graders, and young adults. Books from other countries, cultures, viewpoints, and storytelling traditions can open up a universe of possibility, and the wider our view, the more powerfully books enrich and expand us. In an increasingly complex, globalized world, stories are potent vehicles of empathy. We believe it is essential to teach our kids to place themselves in the shoes of others beyond their communities, and instill in them a lifelong curiosity about the world and their place in it. Through publishing a diverse array of transporting stories, Yonder nurtures the next generation of savvy global citizens and lifelong readers.